No. 13.
Be Brave, Little Noddy!

THIS BOOK
BELONGS TO

Richard

SBN 361 00414 1

MADE AND PRINTED IN GREAT BRITAIN BY PURNELL AND SONS, LTD.,
PAULTON (SOMERSET) AND LONDON

BE BRAVE LITTLE NODDY!

BY

Enid Blyton

CONTENTS

LONDON
SAMPSON LOW, MARSTON & CO., LTD.
AND RICHARDS PRESS LTD.

WHAT A FINE TIME THE NOAH'S ARK MONKEY
IS HAVING!

6

1. ROUND THE CORNER

NODDY was feeling very happy. He had
had such a good morning in his little car!

"My pockets are jingling as loudly as my little
bell!" he said, nodding his head. "What a lot of
passengers I've had to-day!" He put his hand in
his pocket to feel all the money. "First I took
Mr. Wobbly Man to his mother's, and he gave
me a shilling instead of sixpence, because I had to
help him in and out of the car, he's so wobbly!

"Then I took Sailor Doll and his wife to the
station, and that was a shilling too. And then,
when the train came in, there was old Mr. Jumbo
wanting someone to take his luggage for him,
and that was a sixpence for me as well."

He jingled his money again. He really did feel
rich. "I shall buy a chocolate cake and take it up
to Big-Ears' toadstool house for tea," he said, and

sang at the top of his voice as he drove along in his little car.

"A chocolate cake
  I'm going to take
  For Big-Ears' tea,
  How pleased he'll be!"

"Dear me, Noddy, you sound very merry," called Mrs. Noah as he passed. "Stop! I want you to take me to the Ark."

"Oh, hallo, Mrs. Noah," said Noddy, stopping. "Yes—I do feel merry to-day—I've had a very good morning."

"Well, you deserve it, Noddy," said Mrs. Noah, getting in. "You work very hard, and *I* think you're a good driver, though you do knock down lamp-posts sometimes."

"Well, they shouldn't get in my way," said

8

Noddy. "Now where to, Mrs. Noah—the Ark?"

"Yes, please," said Mrs. Noah. "I've been shopping and my parcels are heavy."

"I'm glad I came along then," said Noddy. "I won't charge you anything, Mrs. Noah, because you so often have me to tea!"

But Mrs. Noah wouldn't have her ride for nothing. "No, no," she said. "Here's your sixpence, Noddy—and thank you for helping me."

When he had seen Mrs. Noah safely in the Ark, Noddy felt hungry. "Time for my dinner," he said. "Home, little car, home!"

"Parp-parp!" said the car, pleased, because it had had a long morning and wanted a rest.

Noddy swung round a corner rather fast—and CRASH! He ran right into a car that was parked beside the pavement there. Goodness—what a noise. And what a shock for little Noddy! He was

NODDY FOUND HIMSELF SITTING ON A PILE OF
TOMATOES AND APPLES

shot out of his car, high into the air—and landed on Sid Golly's fruit barrow nearby.

Plonk! Noddy found himself sitting on a pile of tomatoes and apples—and, dear me, quite a lot of them had fallen off the barrow and were rolling in the road!

"Oh, what's happened?" wailed Noddy. "Who's been silly enough to put their car so near the corner?"

It wasn't long before quite a crowd collected round. Sid Golly was very angry about his tomatoes and apples—and, dear me, who was this looking as black as thunder?

It was the man who owned the car. He was a wooden man, but bigger than Noddy, and he wore a gay yellow coat and blue trousers, and a feather in his red hat.

"Now then!" he shouted, shaking his fist at little Noddy. "What's all this?"

2. MR. HONK

NODDY slid off the fruit barrow and went to his own little car. "Oh, it's hurt!" he cried. "Look, the bonnet is broken—and one of the lamps is smashed. Oh, little car, do you feel all right?"

"Poooop," said the car, in a very small voice.

"Can't you say 'Parp-parp', little car?" asked Noddy, anxiously, and pressed the hooter. It was no good—it could only say a very soft "Pooooop!"

"Who cares about your silly car!" said the angry man. "You might have smashed mine to bits. I'll report you!"

"Now then, now then," said a very deep voice, and up came Mr. Plod the policeman, taking out his notebook as he came. "What's happening here?"

"Ha—Mr. Plod!" said the angry man. "I'm Mr. Honk from Toy-Car Town. I parked my car there—see—and round the corner came this red and yellow car, at sixty miles an hour . . ."

"I didn't, I didn't, I didn't!" cried Noddy. "Oooh, what a storyteller! Mr. Plod, I . . ."

"Now, now—one at a time," said Mr. Plod. "Mr. Honk—what damage is done to your car?"

"I DIDN'T damage his car!" said Noddy, his head nodding up and down so fast that it was quite

difficult to see it. "It's such a big car, look—and mine's a little one. *My* car is the one that got hurt."

"WILL you be quiet, Noddy!" said Mr. Plod. "I'm talking to Mr. Honk.

13

Mr. Honk—if any damage is done to your car Noddy will have to pay for it."

"I should think so!" said Mr. Honk, still looking very fierce.

"But, Mr. Plod—I was on my correct side, and

how could I know that Mr. Honk had parked his car *just* round the corner?" wept Noddy, very upset to see his car so hurt. "You *know* it's not right to do that, you know it isn't."

"Noddy's right!" called a voice. It was Miss

Fluffy Cat. "No one should put a car almost on a corner."

"Well," said Mr. Plod, "well, perhaps, Mr. Honk, it would have been better if you . . ."

"Now don't you bother about this, Mr. Plod," said Mr. Honk, hurriedly. "I don't want Noddy to be punished. We'll say no more about it. In fact I'll tow Noddy's car to the garage. I can't say fairer than that."

"Well," said Mr. Plod again, "I suppose that's all right. After all, your car *hasn't* been damaged —but it *would* have been better if you had put . . ."

"Yes, yes, yes," said Mr. Honk, getting into his car. "Noddy, have you a rope? Tie your car on to mine and I'll give you a tow."

Noddy was surprised that the angry Mr. Honk was now being so kind. He didn't know that Mr. Honk was afraid that Mr. Plod was changing his

mind about the accident and might be going to
blame *him* for it, because his car had been parked
so near the corner.

Poor Noddy found a rope and tied the front of
his little car to the back of Mr. Honk's shiny big
one. "Poooooop!" said the little car, softly and
sadly. Noddy patted its bonnet, and felt sad too.

Then he got into the car, and took the steering-
wheel. "I'm ready!" he called to Mr. Honk, and
off they went, Noddy's car wobbling as it ran along
behind.

They came to the garage and Mr. Honk got out.
"What are you?" he asked Noddy. "A taxi-driver?"

"Yes," said Noddy, his head nodding fast.

"I shouldn't think you earn much money,
taking passengers in that silly little car," said Mr.
Honk. "Now a car like mine—big, shiny, fast—
that's the kind to have!"

16

NODDY'S CAR WOBBLED ALONG AS IT RAN BEHIND MR.
HONK'S BIG SHINY CAR

17

"I earn a *lot* of money!" said Noddy, indignantly, and he put his hand into his pocket and pulled out all his shillings and sixpences. "See— that is what I've already earned to-day. And I don't like *your* car very much—it's tinny, and it goes by clockwork. Mine goes properly."

Mr. Honk was staring at all the money Noddy had shown him. "Dear me—it must be easy to get rich here," he said. "Well, I'm afraid you won't be able to take passengers in your car for some time, little nodding man—and it's your own fault!"

"It isn't!" cried Noddy. "You heard what Mr. Plod said—you ought to have put your car farther up the road, not on the corner; you ought to . . ."

But Mr. Honk had jumped into his big car and was driving off fast, laughing. Horrid Mr. Honk! Noddy stared after him and heard Mr. Honk hooting as he went round a corner—Honk! Honk! Honk!

18

3. BE BRAVE, LITTLE NODDY!

POOR little Noddy! He felt very unhappy as he looked at his car. Mr. Golly, who owned the garage, came up to have a look too.

"This will cost you a lot of money, Noddy," he said, "and it will take rather a long time to mend."

Noddy's head nodded sadly. "I thought so," he said. "And it wasn't my fault, you know. Never mind—I must get some other work to do."

"I'll get it done as soon as I can," said Mr. Golly. "Dear me—we *shall* miss having a taxi to take us here, there and everywhere."

Noddy didn't want to go back to his little house. All he wanted was to find Big-Ears and be comforted. So he trudged all the way through the wood to Big-Ears' house. Big-Ears was sitting by the fire, with his cat on his knees. He was most surprised to see such a miserable little Noddy.

"What's the matter?" he said.

"Big-Ears—oh, Big-Ears!" said Noddy, trying to find his hanky. "Oh, Big-Ears!"

"Good gracious—*what's* happened?" said Big-Ears, and pushed his cat off his knees. "Come here and tell me!"

And soon Noddy was pouring out all that had happened. Big-Ears listened in surprise.

"Well, well—what bad luck, Noddy!" he said. "Still, it might have been worse. You might have been badly hurt, and Sid Golly might have made you pay for his fruit. Mr. Plod might even have put you into prison. Cheer up!"

"I can't cheer up," said Noddy.

"Yes you can," said Big-Ears. "You're going to have some fun finding all kinds of new jobs to do till your car is mended, and you're going to show everyone how plucky you are, and how you can laugh when things go wrong!"

"Am I?" said Noddy.

"Of course you are!" said Big-Ears. "Now, let's make up a Brave Song—you're good at making up songs, Noddy. Think of a really nice Brave Song."

"I can't," said Noddy, his head nodding sadly. "You're going to be disappointed in me, Big-Ears. I don't feel very brave about this. I keep remembering my poor little car and how it can only say 'Poooooooop!' instead of 'parp-parp'. Oh, Big-Ears—it did sound so sad!"

Big-Ears didn't take any notice of all this. He began beating time with his right hand and singing.

"De-dee, de-dee, de-dee-dee-dee," he sang, to Noddy's astonishment. "Now let me see—how would a Brave Song go?

Oh, what does it matter if things go wrong,

I'll sing and I'll whistle . . .

Dear, dear, I'm not at all good at making up songs."

"I know how that ought to go," said Noddy,

21

cheering up. "Like this, Big-Ears—you just listen."
And he nodded his head and sang:

"Oh, what does it matter
If things go wrong,
I'll sing and I'll whistle
The whole day long.
I'll go on smiling,
I'll laugh, ho ho!
And brave as a soldier
You'll see me go.
My head is a-nodding,
My little bell rings,
My feet are a-dancing
As if they had wings.
Oh, WHAT DOES IT MATTER
If things go wrong,
I'll sing and I'll whistle
My Brave Little Song!"

Noddy sang this
very loudly in his little
high voice, and he
danced all round Big-
Ears as he sang, nod-
ding his head till his
bell jingled quite
madly.

NODDY SANG VERY LOUDLY IN HIS LITTLE
HIGH VOICE

23

Big-Ears clapped and clapped when Noddy had finished. "Fine, fine!" he said. "The best song you've ever thought of, little Noddy. Why, look —you've even made my old cat dance!"

"Oh, Cat—come and dance with *me*," said Noddy. "Big-Ears and I will sing the Brave Song again, and you can meow. Give me your front paws, Cat."

And there was little Noddy dancing round with the big old cat, singing with Big-Ears at the top of his voice. Really, as Big-Ears said, it was enough to make a cat laugh—and certainly *his* cat was smiling all over its whiskery face!

'I feel better now, Big-Ears," said Noddy, sitting down to get his breath. "That's a good song, isn't it—I'll sing it whenever I feel sad."

"That's right," said Big-Ears. "Face up to trouble, little Noddy, and it will run away—but if *you* run away, trouble will come after you. Now —let's make plans."

4. NODDY FINDS SOME WORK

BIG-EARS was a very, very good friend. He got out a plate of cakes, and a bottle of raspberry syrup made from his own raspberries. Noddy beamed all over his face.

"This makes me feel better too," he said, taking a cake. "Now—what other job shall I do, Big-Ears, till my car is mended?"

"I'll lend you my bicycle," said Big-Ears, "and we'll tie a little wooden cart behind it, Noddy— and you can deliver all kinds of things for the people in Toy Village."

"Oh, Big-Ears—what a very good idea!" said Noddy, munching his cake. "I shall like that. Will you *really* lend me your bicycle? What will you do without it?"

"I'll manage," said Big-Ears, and his face looked so kind that Noddy got up and gave him a big hug.

"I'll give you half the money I earn," said Noddy, his head nodding hard. "And I'll keep your bicycle as clean as I can."

"Let's go and get it now," said Big-Ears. "Dear me, surely you don't want *another* cake, Noddy—that's your fourth."

"Oh dear—you're too good at counting, Big-Ears," said Noddy. "Yes--let's get your bicycle."

Well, it wasn't long before Noddy was riding gaily through the wood on Big-Ears' bicycle. When two small rabbits got in his way he rang the bicycle bell and then he felt sad because it said "R-r-r-r-ring, r-r-r-r-ring!" instead of "Parp-parp!" as his little car-hooter did.

"Now, now—I must remember my Brave Song," said Noddy, and he sang it in time to his pedalling.

"Oh, what does it matter
If things go wrong,
I'll sing and I'll whistle
The whole day long!"

Noddy had quite a good time for the rest of that day. Everyone was most surprised to see him on Big-Ears' bicycle, and when he explained that the little cart was for carrying things to and fro for people till his car was mended, they were all very kind.

Mrs. Tubby Bear was the first to give him a job. "Look," she said, "I've just finished doing some washing for old Miss Golly. Take it in your little cart for me, Noddy. She will give you some money and you can keep sixpence of it for yourself."

"Oh, thank you, Mrs. Tubby Bear!" said Noddy, very pleased. He put the basket into the little cart, got on the bicycle, and away he went. It was rather hard work pedalling up the hill to Miss Golly's, but never mind—he had his Brave Song to sing!

"I simply mustn't forget that," said Noddy to himself. "I still keep feeling sad, so I must sing the Brave Song as often as I can. And this evening I'll go and see my little car and sing it the Brave Song to cheer it up, because I expect it's feeling rather sad too."

The car was very glad when Noddy rode into the garage on Big-Ears' bicycle. "Pooooooooop!" it said, and jiggled up and down a little. Noddy patted its bonnet and then he danced round it and sang the Brave Song. The car joined in with a few little "Pooooooooops".

Mr. Golly smiled at Noddy. "I'm doing my best to mend your car quickly," he said. "I'm glad to see you're being so brave about it, Noddy."

"Big-Ears made me brave," said Noddy. "I'm not *really* a very brave person, Mr. Golly. I could quite easily burst into tears when I look at my poor little car—see, this lamp is quite smashed. Oh dear!"

"Off you go!" said Mr. Golly. "Unless you

want me to use your tears to wash down this car, and save me getting out the hose! Come and cry over this muddy car bonnet and make it nice and wet."

"Now you've made me laugh!" said little Noddy, and he nodded his head and smiled. "Good-bye, Mr. Golly; good-bye, car. I'll come again."

28

NODDY'S CAR JIGGLED UP AND DOWN A LITTLE

"Poooooooop!" said the car, in its new, soft little voice.

Noddy hurried out with Big-Ears' bicycle. "Now —who wants something delivering?" he wondered, and he rang the bell gaily, and sang loudly:

> "Hallo, hallo,
> Does anybody
> Want some help
> From little Noddy?
> Parcels carried
> Here and there,
> Shopping fetched
> From anywhere!"

5. A DREADFUL SHOCK

NEXT day Noddy cleaned Big-Ears' bicycle before he set out with the little cart behind.

"Bicycle, I'll clean you well,
Handle-bars and wheels and bell,
Then I'll pedal you away
And earn my living all the day!"

sang Noddy as he polished and rubbed. Mrs. Tubby Bear heard him and looked over the wall.

"You're a good little Noddy," she said. "Why don't you go to the Noah's Ark this morning and ask Mrs. Noah if you can do her shopping for her? It's her busy day to-day, and she could give you her shopping list and you could bring everything back to the Ark in that little cart."

"Oh, what a good idea!" said Noddy, and jumped on to the bicycle at once. Away he went, with the little cart trailing behind.

Mrs. Noah was very pleased to see him. It was her washing day and little Noddy could hardly see her, there was so much soapy lather in the tub.

"If you've got your shopping list, I'll go to the shops for you and bring everything back," said Noddy, nodding his head.

"Well, well—to think you've got Big-Ears' bicycle and little cart!" said Mrs. Noah. "And you're getting all kinds of jobs till your little car is mended, I hear. You're a good brave little Noddy, because we all know it wasn't *your* fault that your car was damaged!"

"No, it wasn't," said Noddy. "It was Mr. Honk's fault—and he never even said he was sorry. But never mind, it will soon be mended and then I can be your taxi-driver again!"

He took Mrs. Noah's list, and off he went. He didn't see that one of the Noah's Ark monkeys had leapt into the little cart behind—look what a fine time he's having!

"Dear me—the cart's very heavy to pull!" said Noddy, panting, and looked round. "Oh—you bad monkey! I'll take you straight to Mr. Plod!"

But the monkey jumped out at once, and leapt up to the roof of a house. So Noddy couldn't get him. He pedalled on, and then, coming down the middle of the road, he saw a big shiny car that swept by and almost knocked Noddy into the gutter.

On the front of the car was a notice —and what *do* you think it said? Here it is:

TAXI FOR HIRE
SIXPENCE A
TIME

Noddy couldn't believe his eyes! He got off the bicycle and stared after the car. He knew that car—and he knew the driver!

"Why—that was Mr. Honk!" said Noddy. "Good gracious me! MR. HONK! And he's using his car as a taxi—in Toyland Village too, where *I'm* the taxi-driver!"

The big shiny car stopped and picked up the Sailor Doll and his wife and little boy. It was such a big car that it could easily take them all. Then off it went again, and Noddy could hear it hooting proudly.

"Honk! Honk! Honk!"

Suddenly Noddy wasn't brave any more. He sat down on the kerb by the gutter and wailed loudly, the tears splashing round his feet.

"It's Mr. Honk! He made me have an accident

because he parked his car near a corner—and now while my car's being mended *he's* being a taxi-driver! And his car is MUCH bigger; he'll take all my passengers and I'll NEVER be a taxi-driver again!"

34

THE BIG SHINY CAR PICKED UP SAILOR DOLL AND HIS
WIFE AND LITTLE BOY

Just at that moment Mrs. Tubby Bear came by —and she was most surprised to see Noddy sitting on the kerb with tears rolling down his cheeks.

"Why, little Noddy—I thought you were so brave!" she said. "Surely you're not crying about your little car!"

"I'm c-c-crying because Mr. Honk is using his c-c-c-car as a t-t-taxi," wept Noddy. "And I'M the taxi-d-d-d-driver here."

"Get up, Noddy," said Mrs. Tubby Bear. "Don't worry about Mr. Honk. As soon as *ever* your car is mended everyone will let you drive them again—and won't have Mr. Honk."

"Won't they?" said Noddy, standing up, his head nodding sadly. "They might! His is a bigger car than mine and goes very fast."

"Let me wipe your eyes," said Mrs. Tubby Bear. "Now—what about that Brave Song you sang to me yesterday? Get on Big-Ears' bicycle, and ride away singing it. Go along. Come to tea this afternoon and have some of my strawberry jam."

Noddy tried to smile. He got on his bicycle and rode away slowly, trying to sing his Brave Song:

"Oh, what does it matter (sniff-sniff-sniff)
When things go wrong (oh dear, oh dear!)
I'll sing and I'll whistle
The whole day long!" (sniff-sniff-SNIFF!)

But by the time he had got to the end of the song he felt much better, and rang his bell so fiercely at Mr. Wobbly-Man that he wobbled into the middle of a very big puddle and got stuck there.

"That horrid Mr. Honk," said Noddy, as he cycled off to do Mrs. Noah's shopping. "Mean Mr. Honk! I don't LIKE Mr. Honk! But oh dear—I expect he's a very, very good taxi-driver!"

6. GOOD NEWS!

NODDY was very busy that day and the next. He did the shopping for a great many people and trundled it home for them in the little cart, which quite enjoyed itself, jerking and jolting down the road, jiggling everywhere behind Noddy.

"I take your parcel
And your bundle
And my little cart I trundle!" sang Noddy.
"And I'll quickly
Do your shopping—
See me cycle without stopping!
I am trusty,
Safe and steady,
Always quick and always ready!"

"Have you heard Noddy's new little song?" said Miss Fluffy Cat to Mr. Monkey. "Really, he's a good little fellow, you know—and very brave about the accident to his little car."

"Yes. He took all my potatoes to market for me and never dropped one," said Monkey. "*And* he stood there and sold them for me. By the way —have you seen Mr. Honk's taxi? It's very grand indeed."

"Yes, I've seen it," said Miss Fluffy Cat. "Well, I shall use it till Noddy's car comes back from the garage, but after that I shall have Noddy again. We shan't want Mr. Honk then."

"No, of course we shan't," said Monkey. "He'll have to go somewhere else then. We don't need *two* taxi-drivers in Toy Village."

Noddy went to see his little car quite often, and it always said "Poooooop" as soon as he walked into the garage. But one evening it said "Parp-parp" in its old voice, and Noddy jumped for joy.

"Oh! You can say 'Parp-parp' again, little

car," he said. "Are you feeling better?"

"Parp-parp-PARP!" said the little car and jiggled up and down on its four wheels.

"Your bonnet's mended," said Noddy, "and you have a new lamp. You want some new paint, then you'll be ready for me to drive again!"

"I'm going to paint your car this evening," said Mr. Golly. "It will be ready to-morrow—but there's rather a big bill to pay, Noddy."

"You can have half the money I've been earning with Big-Ears' bicycle and little cart," said Noddy, happily. "And if that's not enough I'll soon earn some more."

"If Mr. Honk stays on here in Toy Village with his car *you* won't earn very much," said Mr. Golly.

"Oh, but he's sure to go as soon as *my* car's back again!" said Noddy. "Oh, I do feel happy to think I'll soon drive my little car once more. Aren't *you* happy, little car?"

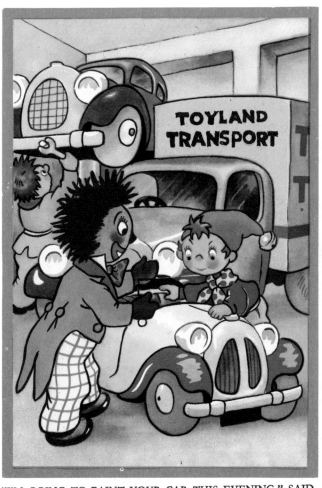

"I'M GOING TO PAINT YOUR CAR THIS EVENING," SAID
MR. GOLLY

"Parp-parp-PARP!" said the little car, and jiggled again.

"Well, good-bye now," said Noddy. "I'll come and fetch you tomorrow, little car. I'll take Big-Ears' bicycle and cart back to him now, and stay the night with him—and then I'll fetch you tomorrow morning."

And off he went for the last time on Big-Ears' bicycle, with the little cart trundling merrily after him. He came to Big-Ears' toadstool house and rang the bicycle bell loudly.

"Big-Ears, Big-Ears!" he cried. "I've good news! Open the door quickly and let me in!"

7. PARP-PARP-PARP!

BIG-EARS was very pleased to hear all that Noddy had to say. He was glad to see Noddy so happy and to hear his bell tinkling so gaily.

"This evening I'm going to clean your bicycle very, very well for the last time, Big-Ears," said Noddy. "And then I shall count out half my money for you for lending it to me. You are a good friend to me, Big-Ears, and I love you very much."

"Well, you've been very brave about everything, little Noddy," said Big-Ears, pleased. "Especially when you saw that horrid Mr. Honk taking your place as taxi-driver in Toy Village. That was a mean thing to do. People don't like him very much, you know."

"Why don't they?" asked Noddy, in surprise.

"He drives much too fast, and he won't always carry people's baggage for them," said Big-Ears. "And he isn't very polite. Ah well— he won't be here much longer. You'll be our taxi-driver to-morrow."

Noddy cleaned Big-Ears' bicycle and the little cart too. Then he counted out half the money he had earned and gave it to Big-Ears, and put the other half away for Mr. Golly at the garage.

"Now we'll go to bed," said Big-Ears. "And to-morrow when you wake up you'll feel very, very happy!"

44

"I'll set the alarm clock for seven o'clock," said Noddy, sleepily. "Then I shall be able to go and fetch my car as soon as the garage opens. Good night, Big-Ears. What about the cat? It's right in the middle of my bed, and it won't move."

Big-Ears made a squeak just like a mouse, and you should have seen the cat leap off the bed at once and go sniffing into the corners. That made Noddy laugh and his little bell ring.

"You are so clever, Big-Ears," he said. "Cat, don't you dare to jump on my middle when I'm asleep! See you to-morrow morning at seven o'clock, Big-Ears!"

But Noddy heard something else before the alarm went off at seven o'clock! At just five minutes to seven something ran right up to the front door of Big-Ears' house—and then there came a sound that Noddy knew very well indeed!

"Parp. Parp-parp-PARP!"

Noddy woke up with a jump and leapt out of bed, shouting. "It's my little car! It wouldn't wait for me to fetch it. It's come to find me!"

And sure enough it *was* his little car! It had shot out of the garage as soon as Mr. Golly had opened the doors, and had gone all the way to the Toadstool House by itself.

46

"IT'S MY LITTLE CAR!" SHOUTED NODDY. "IT'S COME
TO FIND ME!"

47

Noddy ran to it and sat in the driver's seat. He drove up and down the woodland path, hooting madly, and all the little rabbits peeped out to see whatever could be happening!

"It's Noddy and his car," they told one another. "He's got his car again. Listen!"

"Parp-parp-parp-parpparp!" Yes, everyone knew that Noddy had his little car again and would soon be going down to Toyland Village to pick up passengers as usual.

8. HONK! HONK!

BIG-EARS and Noddy had a very quick breakfast and then Noddy drove down to the village to show everyone that he was back again Mrs. Tubby Bear was very pleased when he stopped and hooted outside her house.

"Oh—there's Noddy and his car again!" she said. "We must get him to take us to the station this morning to meet your brother, Tubby Bear."

"We will," said Tubby Bear, and called out to tell Noddy. Noddy's head nodded happily.

"Yes, yes—I'll fetch you in plenty of time," he said. "I'm just taking Mr. Toy Dog to the barber's to have his whiskers cut."

"Parp-parp-parp!" Everyone was pleased to hear that sound again. Noddy was very happy indeed. He took Mr. Toy Dog to the barber and then he went to fetch the Tubby Bears to take them to the station to meet Mr. Tubby's brother.

Mrs. Tubby Bear couldn't find her purse, so they were rather late in starting—and oh, what a DREADFUL shock Noddy had when they reached the station!

Mr. Honk was there with his big, shiny car—and he had got Mr. Tubby Bear's brother in his car, and was driving him out of the station yard to Mr. Tubby's house.

"Hey!" cried Noddy, indignantly. "What are you doing, taking passengers when *I'm* back again, Mr. Honk? How dare you! I'm the taximan for this village."

"Honk, honk!" hooted Mr. Honk's car and swept so near Noddy's that Noddy had to wrench his wheel round to get out of the way.

"Ha ha, ho ho!" laughed Mr. Honk. "*I'm* the taximan now, Noddy—and you can't do anything about it!" And away he went with Tubby Bear's brother.

"What a horrid fellow!" said Mrs. Tubby Bear. "Oh, Noddy—I do so hope he won't stay here. He'll be meeting all the trains and taking your passengers."

Noddy was most alarmed. Nobody could make Mr. Honk go away if he wanted to stay, that

was certain. Not even Mr. Plod the policeman.

Noddy began to wail. "His car is bigger than mine! It takes more passengers. It goes faster. Whatever am I to do?"

"Now, now, Noddy, don't wail like that," said Mr. Tubby Bear. "Let's go back to your house and ask Big-Ears what to do—you left him there this morning, didn't you?"

"Yes, I did," said Noddy. "We'll go back to him. Oh dear—Mr. Honk will be just outside your house, Mr. Tubby Bear, because he's taken your brother there, and he'll hoot at me again."

Off they went to Noddy's house and found Big-Ears standing in the front garden looking in surprise at Mr. Honk's car. Mr. Honk had just gone indoors with Tubby Bear's brother, carrying some of his luggage and hoping for a good tip.

"Big-Ears, Big-Ears, Mr. Honk says he won't go away!" shouted Noddy, almost tumbling out of his car. "What shall I do? Oh, I'm so miserable!"

"Now then—what about your Brave Song?" said Big-Ears, looking quite stern. "Go indoors, Noddy, and sing it at the top of your voice—and then come out here. I promise you that everything will be quite all right then."

"Oh, Big-Ears—whatever do you mean?" said Noddy in surprise. He went into his little House-For-One and shut the door. He stood in the middle of the floor and sang loudly:

52

"NOW THEN—WHAT ABOUT YOUR BRAVE SONG?" SAID
BIG-EARS TO NODDY QUITE STERNLY

"Oh, what does it matter
If things go wrong,
I'll sing and I'll whistle
The whole day long!

(Can I come out now, Big-Ears? No? All right,
I'll sing again.)

I'll go on smiling
I'll laugh, ho ho!
And brave as a soldier
You'll see me go.
My head is a-nodding,
My little bell rings,
My feet are a-dancing
As if they had wings.
Oh, WHAT DOES IT MATTER
If things go wrong,
I'll sing and I'll whistle
My Brave Little Song!"

9. BIG-EARS IS VERY CLEVER

THEN out marched Noddy bravely with a smile on his face. "Did you hear me?" he asked. "I feel better again now. What have you been doing, Big-Ears? You said you'd make everything all right."

"Sh!" said Big-Ears, as Mr. Honk came striding out of Mr. Tubby Bear's house next door, jingling some money. He grinned rudely at Noddy.

"You may as well give up!" he said. "I tell you, *I'm* the taximan now! Who wants to ride in your silly little car when they can hire my lovely big shiny one?"

"It's a horrid car!" shouted Noddy. "A tinny one—just a clock-work one!"

Mr. Honk got into his car and hooted his

horn loudly to drown what Noddy was saying.
Then he drove off, and Noddy watched him go,
feeling very sad. He turned to Big-Ears.

"But, Big-Ears," he said, in rather a wobbly
voice, "you said—you did say—you'd make things
all right! And you haven't!"

"Oh, haven't I?" said Big-Ears, with the biggest
smile Noddy had ever seen on his face before.
"Well—look here!"

And Big-Ears held out his hand—and in it
was a big clockwork key! Yes—the key to
Mr. Honk's car!

"Ooooh! BIG-EARS! Why—it's the key of that clockwork car!" cried Noddy. "Oooooh! When the car runs down he won't be able to wind it up again—so it won't go."

"It certainly won't!" said Big-Ears, beaming. "It serves him right. Damaging your car—and taking your job—and being so rude as well! I won't have it!"

"Oh, Big-Ears—but what will he *say*?" cried Noddy, his eyes shining. "He'll guess it's you."

"Yes—of course," said Big-Ears. "And he'll come back and demand his key—and he shall have it too, *if* he promises to go right away and never come back!"

"Big-Ears, you are the cleverest person I know!" said Noddy, and he gave him such a hug that Big-Ears quite lost his breath. "Oh, Big-Ears, whatever should I do without you? Quick—let's go to the ice-cream shop and see if it's open. Come on, little car—I like your parp-parp much better than that horrid honk-honk!"

And away they go together, with Noddy singing loudly:

58

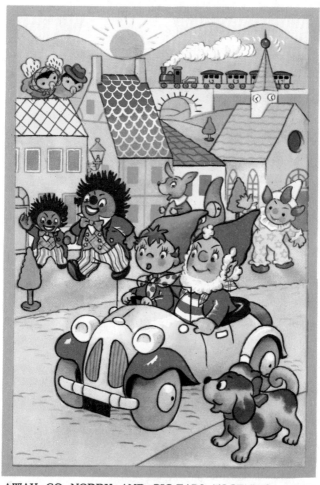

AWAY GO NODDY AND BIG-EARS TOGETHER, WITH
NODDY SINGING LOUDLY

"Oh, what does it matter
If things go wrong,
I've only to wait
Till my friend comes along.
(Parp-parp-parp!)
He's kind and he's clever,
His name you all know,
And this song is to tell you
I do love him so!
(Parp-parp-parp!)"

"Look—look!" said Big-Ears, pointing ahead. "Mr. Honk's car has run down already. Oh, Noddy —*now* we're going to have some fun!"

So they are—but really I don't feel a BIT sorry for that horrid Mr. Honk!